For Kieron and Jermaine T.C.
For Joseph A.A.

First published in hardback in Great Britain by HarperCollins Publishers Ltd in 2000
First published in paperback by Collins Picture Books in 2001

1 3 5 7 9 10 8 6 4 2
ISBN: 0 00 664621 2

Collins Picture Books is an imprint of the Children's Division, part of HarperCollins Publishers Ltd.
Text copyright © Trish Cooke 2000
Illustrations copyright © Alex Ayliffe 2000

The HarperCollins website address is:
www.**fire**and**water**.com

Printed in Singapore.

Zoom!

Trish Cooke
illustrated by Alex Ayliffe

Collins

An imprint of HarperCollinsPublishers

Hurricane Kieron and Rush Around Ria
were brother and sister.
Trouble was...

they were always in a hurry.
They just could not keep still.
They never walked anywhere.
They always ran.

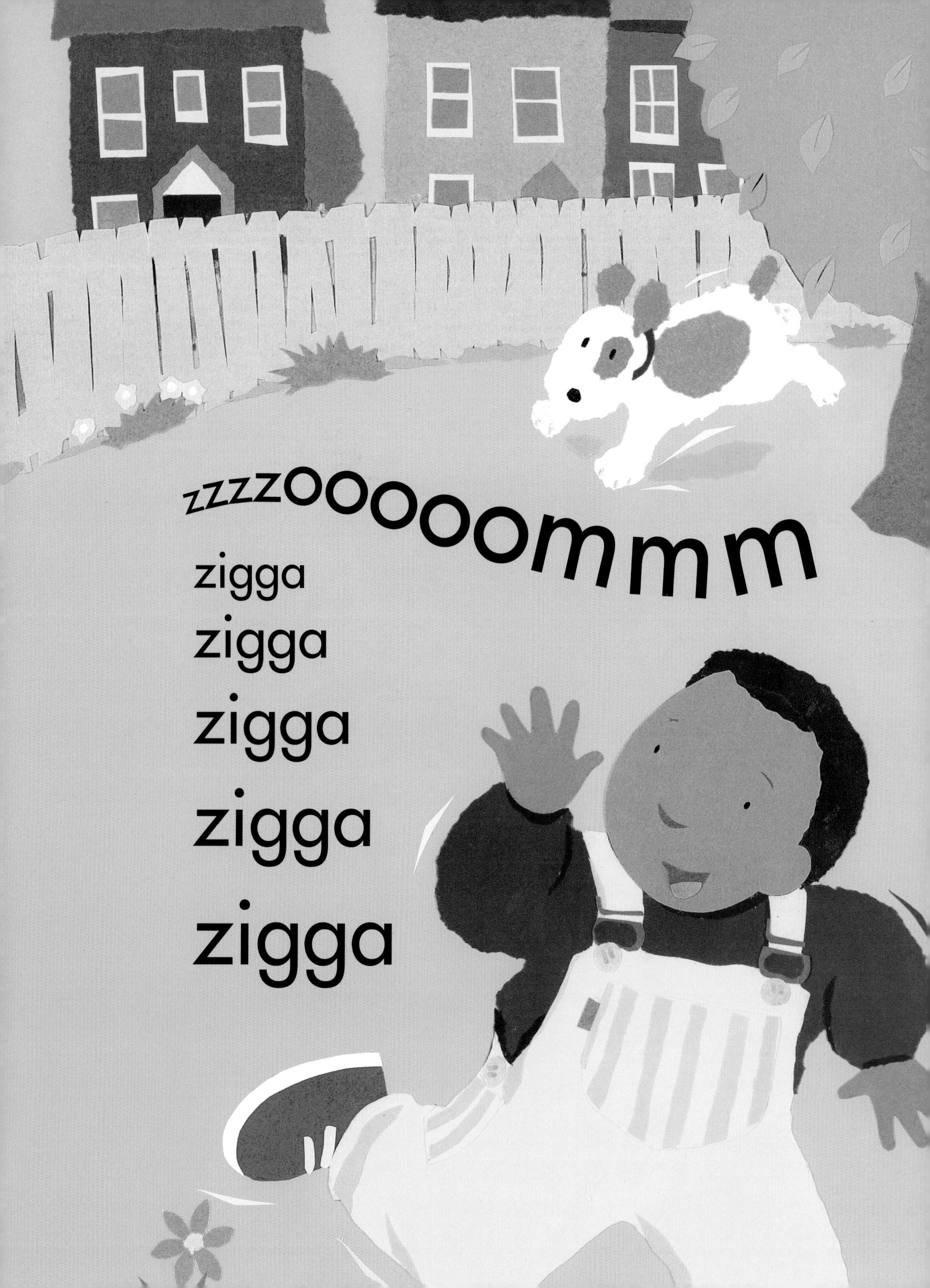

zzzzooooommmm

zigga

zigga

zigga

zigga

zigga

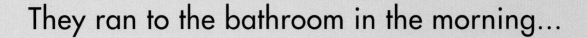

They ran to the bathroom in the morning...

wheeeeeeee!

Aaaaaaagh!

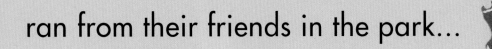

ran from their friends in the park...

Help!

Can't Catch Me!

ran just for the sake of it...

Yow! Yow! Yow!

ran down the stairs... oops!

ran on the spot...

Left Right Left Right

ran round and round...

and round...

whoooooiwheee

Trouble was they only stopped...

Uh huh!

when it was time for bed...

Phew!

But, come the morning, they
would start all over again.

Then one day, right, Hurricane Kieron
fell and cut his knee and he cried and
cried and cried.

And then he stopped crying and he tried
to run again. But he couldn't because
it HURT! So he sat down again.
But Rush Around Ria didn't wait for
him – she just carried on running.

And he watched and he watched
but he couldn't join in and
Rush Around Ria carried
on without him.

It didn't matter to her that he couldn't
join in, least not at first... But then...

Hurricane Kieron found something else to do.
Something he had to sit quietly to do.

Something which meant no running around.
Something he had to think about.

So when Rush Around Ria rushed around,
Kieron did not notice. He was too busy,
busy painting pictures...

Hurricane pictures!

He didn't have to zoom to make a hurricane now. All he had to do was mix the paint and he could make a zzzzooooommm on the paper.

First red then blue then orange and green
and purple and yellow and brown and black.
And Rush Around Ria kept rushing back
to see what Kieron was up to.

Then Ria took a paint brush and painted
a rushhhhhhhh. Whoosh
Whoosh
Whoosh

So with rushes and hurricanes the paper got wetter. And after a few days Hurricane Kieron got better. Better enough to run around with Ria...

If they wanted to...

Little Pig Figwort

HENRIETTA BRANFORD
ILLUSTRATED BY
CLAUDIO MUÑOZ

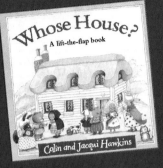

Whose House?

A lift-the-flap book

Colin and Jacqui Hawkins

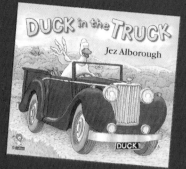

DUCK in the TRUCK

Jez Alborough

DUCK 1

WHERE'S TIM'S TED?

Ian Whybrow
Illustrated by Russell Ayto

Every child deserves the best...

Mucky pup

KEN BROWN

I Love You, Blue Kangaroo!

EMMA CHICHESTER CLARK

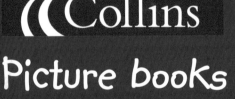

Collins

Picture books

The Tiger Who Came to Tea

JUDITH KERR

THE SECOND PRINCESS

2

Hiawyn Oram and Tony Ross

Nosy Rosy

She just can't help sticking her nose in...

Peter Curry

Snore!

Michael Rosen & Jonathan Langley